▲▼▲

▼▲▼

STORY

BY

RAFE

MARTIN

▲▼▲

▼▲▼

PICTURES

BY

DAVID

SHANNON

▲▼▲

▼▲▼

SCHOLASTIC INC.

NEW YORK TORONTO LONDON
AUCKLAND SYDNEY
MEXICO CITY NEW DELHI
HONG KONG BUENOS AIRES

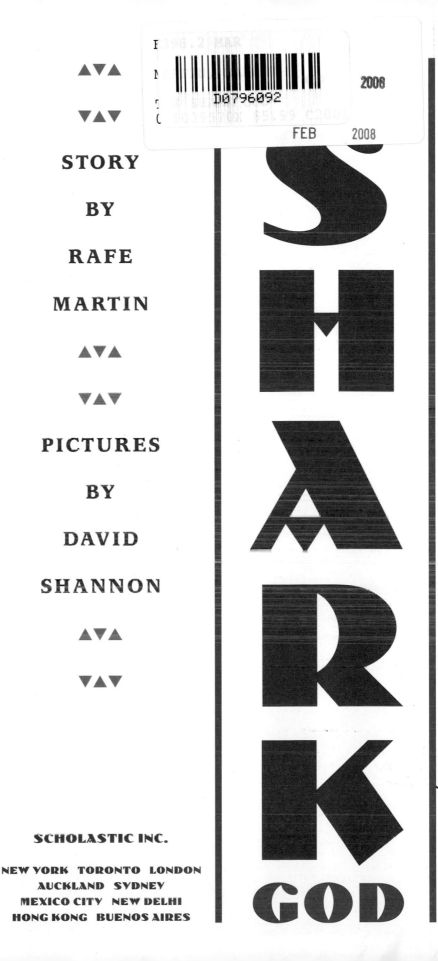

SHARK GOD

IT WAS LONG, LONG AGO that two children, a brother and sister, tried to find someone to help them save a shark.

They ran home, but neither their father nor mother were there.

"Why should I care about a fish?" laughed a woman they met.

"Don't bother us with nonsense," snarled one of the king's counselors at the palace gate.

"A shark?" exclaimed a third man, grabbing his spear. "Lead me to it. I'll kill it."

So the boy and girl climbed down the cliff themselves to where the shark lay entangled and thrashing in the shallows.

"*Mano*," the girl called gently, "we mean no harm."

"Yes," said the boy. "We only want to free you."

Strangely, the shark seemed to understand, for it stopped struggling and lay calmly, watching them with its round, black eyes.

At last, the final coil of tangled rope fell away. Unbound, the shark swam off, its fin cutting the waves like a blade. Where the sea turned dark blue it paused, raised its head from the water, looked back at the children, then sank and was gone.

Laughing and shouting, the children raced along the beach, elated. They'd done it!

On their way back through the village, they passed the king's drum. It was *kapu*, forbidden for anyone but the king to touch it. But no one was there, and oh how they wanted to drum out their triumph! The king glanced from his window and saw them approach. His eyes narrowed. His lips grew tight. He might have called, "Stop! Remember, it is *kapu*!" But he just watched, saying nothing.

The children stepped closer. They looked. They reached out — and lightly touched the drum. Such a soft sound it made, like the faintest patter of summer rain on green leaves far, far away.

But the king saw — and he heard. "Guards!" he shouted.
"Take them!"
The guards ran and grabbed the children.

The parents hurried to the palace and prostrated themselves before the king. "Great King," pleaded the father. "Please. Free my boy and girl."

"Great King, remember," begged the mother. "They are but children. Children must learn."

"Silence!" bellowed the king. "They have broken my law. In three days they shall die. That is justice."

"Alas," wept the parents. "Who can help us?"

The parents left the palace. To each person they met, they told their tale and asked for help. But no one seemed to care. They all just shrugged and said, "That is how he is. Our king has a hard heart. If you don't like it, you should leave." Then the parents saw that the people of the island had all become as hard-hearted as their king.

Then, for their children's sake, at last they went where no one had ever gone willingly before — into the cavern of Kauhuhu, the fearsome Shark God.

Green waves rolled seething into the cavern, where seaweed lay tangled on the black lava rocks. The salt smell of the sea was strong.

As they entered, fear rose like a wave and washed over them. They ran and hid among the rocks. More water surged into the cavern. With the eighth wave, a huge shark slid onto the beach. The Shark God reared itself up and, before their horrified eyes, transformed into a gigantic man on whose mighty back was the tattoo of open shark's jaws.

"A man!" roared the Shark God, hungrily sniffing the air. "I smell a woman and a man!"

He reached down and lifted the canoe-builder up in one great fist, his wife in the other. "Now," he growled, "I am going to eat you up."

"Great One!" the man cried boldly. "Eat us if you must, but first hear our tale!"

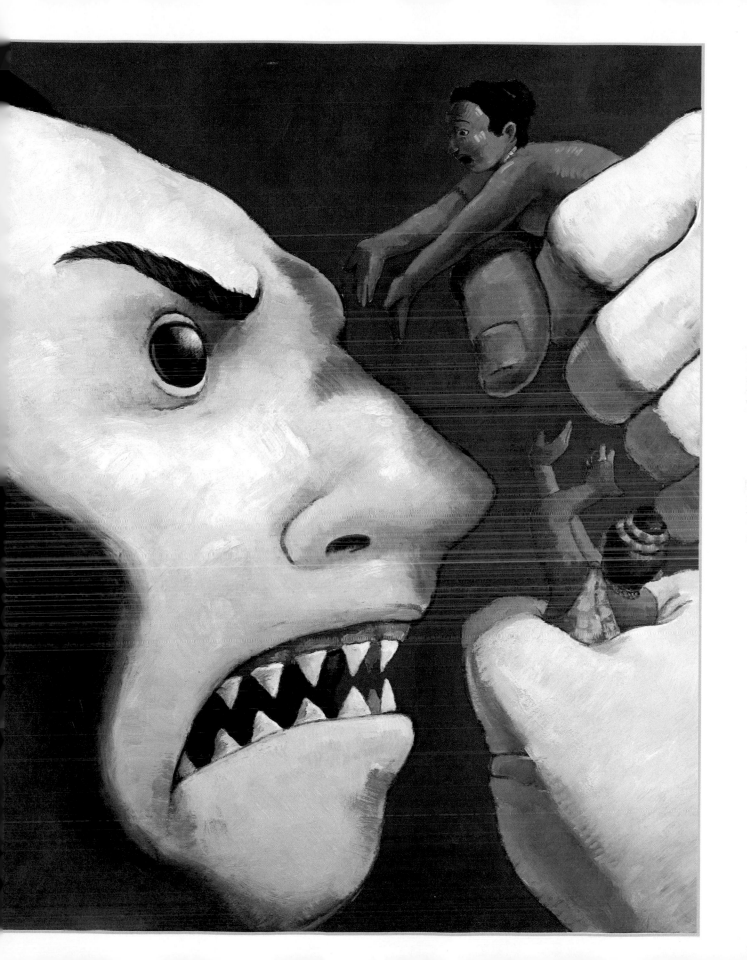

Then, in tears, the parents told of their children's plight. The Shark God listened, nodding his huge head. When they were done, he smiled grimly, showing many strong, sharp, white teeth.

"Prepare a canoe with all you might need for a journey," said the Shark God. "Bring offerings to the temple. Do not fear. I will send a sign. Go out to sea then, and your children will be brought to you."

The parents bowed gratefully and hurried away. They prepared. And they watched and waited. At the dawn of the third day, a rainbow arched from the blue sea and touched the offerings.

Then, far out at sea, a tiny cloud appeared. Larger and larger it grew as it raced toward the island.

The sky grew dark. The wind began to blow. The king looked from his window in alarm. He ran to his drum and beat loudly upon it. Boom! Ba-Boom! The people all hurried to the palace. But the man and his wife went down to the cove, pushed out the canoe, and paddled beyond the reef. There they waited on the rolling sea.

Lightning flashed. Thunder crashed. BOOM! BA-BOOM! A great wave rose. Up and up it rose. It rushed over the land, over the houses and trees, and broke upon the palace, crumpling it to the ground. The children were washed free! They swam to the gate of their prison, which now floated before them, and clambered on. Then an immense shark rose from the dark water and pushed the gate and the children over the flooded land.

Out to sea they traveled, out to the waiting canoe, and into the arms of their mother and father. The great shark lifted its huge head from the water, its sharp, white teeth shining in a grin. For a moment it remained balanced upright, watching them calmly with round, black, wise eyes. Then it sank down and disappeared beneath the waves.

"Great One," chanted the family, "we give you our thanks and shall remember this day always."

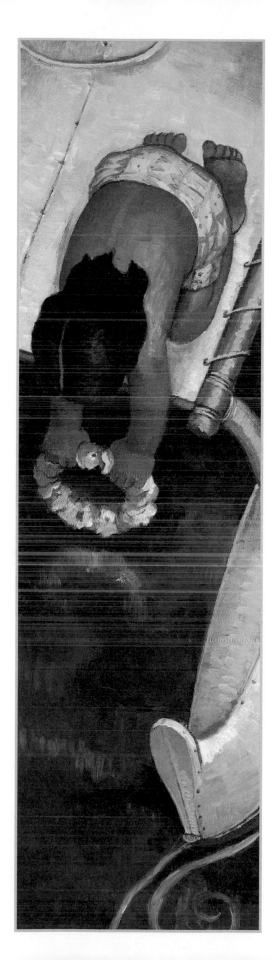

Something red came bobbing on the waves. "Our drum!" shouted the children. They lifted it on board. "Far away, children," said the canoe-builder, "many, many miles across the blue sea, there is another island. The king of that island is kind and just, and the people there still have good hearts. We shall bring the drum to him. *Lele ka hoaka.* Truly, the spirit of this land has flown away."

The wind blew, filling the sail. The drum throbbed, making a sound like laughter among palm trees, like white surf breaking far, far away. Swiftly now they raced over the waves, heading out across the wide ocean toward their new home.

▲▼▲ AUTHOR'S NOTE ▼▲▼

More than twenty years ago, I first came across a version of this story in Padraic Colum's *Legends of Hawaii*. It leapt out at me. As a child I had loved sharks and, though I grew up in New York City, used to make Aqua-Lungs of cardboard and diving masks of rubber and jump out of trees, imagining I was leaping into the ocean.

Years later, I was invited to tell stories at Hawaii's Talking Island Storytelling Festival, and I was able to gather information on sharks as well as on the magnificence of ancient Hawaiian culture, so deeply, spiritually woven into the land itself. Friends there guided me to sources. Martha Beckwith's classic *Hawaiian Mythology* was important, containing information on sharks as *aumakua* or familial totems, as well as a clear synopsis of a version of the traditional tale. Trips to the Bishop Museum on Oahu helped with details. (David Shannon also visited the Bishop Museum while researching the visual details of his pictures.) Westervelt's *Hawaiian Legends of Ghosts and Ghost-Gods* presented a complete version of the story titled, "Kauhuhu, The Shark God of Molokai." Mary Kawena Pukui's *Olelo No'eau: Hawaiian Proverbs and Poetical Sayings* offered delightful background.

Still, could it really be told as a picture book for children today? The changes I made were relatively simple. In the traditional story, the events are spurred on by an execution that cries for vengeance; in my version two children—now a brother and sister instead of two boys—save a shark and are then saved in return. The powerful and solitary *kahuna* (priest)-artist became a husband. And I added the tender figure of a mother as part of this family, while the two lizard watchmen of the Shark God disappeared. The time frame in my version is compressed, months becoming days, so that the children could be saved "in the nick of time." And finally, I added the idea of an island to which the family sails, hoping to fulfill the promise of a new life.

To the Sharks—and their god.
— R. M.

▲▼▲
▼▲▼

To Heidi and Emma, with love.
— D. S.

ISBN-13: 978-0-590-39570-0   ISBN-10: 0-590-39570-X

Text copyright © 2001 by Rafe Martin ▲ Illustrations copyright © 2001 by David Shannon ▲ All rights reserved. Published by Scholastic Inc. SCHOLASTIC, the LANTERN LOGO, and associated logos are trademarks and/or registered trademarks of Scholastic Inc.

Arthur A. Levine Books hardcover edition designed by David Shannon and David Saylor, published by Arthur A. Levine Books, an imprint of Scholastic Inc., October 2001.

12 11 10 9 8 7 6 5 4 3 2 1   7 8 9 10 11 12/0
Printed in the U.S.A. 40 ▲ First Bookshelf edition, June 2007